D1503819

Grandma's Treasure Chest

Written by

Grandma Janet Mary™

with love,
Grandma Janet Mary

Bath Elementary Sch...
Bath, Michigan 48808

Illustrated by

Craig Pennington

4th book in the Grandma Janet Mary™ Series
My Grandma and Me *Publishers*

Acknowledgements

Special thanks to my grandchildren:
Ellen Marie, for her very special contribution to this book,
Maddie Mae, Ethan Jacob, Gavin Randall, Murray Michael, Gabriella K, Maggie Shawn, and Gibson Michael,
for providing me with special inspiration
and to
Greg and Marta Lawrence and my daughter-in-law, Kim Sinke,
who served as advisors, editors and loving supporters.

No part of this book may be reproduced or transmitted in any manner without the
author's expressed written consent. Inquiries about this book should be addressed to:

Grandma Janet Mary
My Grandma and Me Publishers
P.O. Box 144
St. Johns, Michigan 48879
Web site: www.mygrandmaandme.com
E-mail: info@mygrandmaandme.com

First Edition
Printed and bound in Canada
Friesens of Altona, Manitoba

Library of Congress Cataloging-in-Publication Data on File

ISBN 0-9742732-3-6
LCCN 2005904423

*Dedicated to the memory of my dear Grandma Mary Stay
who long ago, on a rainy summer afternoon, took the time
to share with me her priceless treasures.*

I will forever remember.

To grandchildren of all ages,

Old, familiar voices gently calling out your name,
tender moments shared with those
whose smiles remain the same,
holding hands with someone who
will guide you on your way,
your goodness felt in hearts of those
who treasure you each day,
remember then, these special gifts.

Be blessed your whole life through,
and run, don't walk to open arms
waiting just for you.

May your life be filled with treasures such as these.

With love,
Grandma Janet Mary™

My Grandma's swing is creaking
as together, her and I,

take some time
to watch awhile
the changing
bright blue sky,

for darker clouds
are rolling in,
but I don't mind
at all.

And
as I sit here waiting
for the summer rain
to fall,

I wonder
what the day will bring,
and then
it comes to me.

My Grandma
has a treasure chest
that I would love
to see.

She puts her arm around me, says,
"It might just rain all day.
So, tell me child, what should we do?
Let's try and find a way

to make this day a special day."
I smiled because I knew
the perfect way to answer her.
I knew what we could do.

"I have this great idea," I said.
"It's long been on my mind
to peek inside your treasure chest.
It's there I think I'll find

your rubies, em'ralds, silver coins,
long earrings made of gold,
just like the jewels a princess wears
in stories I've been told."

She smiles a knowing kind of smile
I don't quite understand.
She leads me to her bedroom door.
I feel her gentle hand.

"Quite right you are," my Grandma says.
"I'm rich beyond compare
and all the money in the world
can't buy what I will share.

So, sit with me. I'm glad you're here.
We'll spend this day in June
creating brand new mem'ries
while it rains the afternoon."

Her room,
it has a special feel,
the softness of her bed

is neatly covered
with a quilt that's trimmed
with golden thread.

And next to where
she lays her head,
a silver tarnished frame,

still holds the picture
of a bride
whose smile
has stayed the same.

Close by
her wedding picture sits
a worn out
book of prayer

and I can tell
it's all been placed
with tender loving care.

A gentle breeze stirs curtains
that are trimmed with ivory lace.

I look below the window; then,
I smile at Grandma's face,

grape hyacinth

for there it is, her treasure chest.
She whispers, "I believe
that in this life true treasures are
those gifts we do receive

from family, friends, the ones we love,
their mem'ries sweet and warm."
With caring hands she opens it.
The gentle summer storm

still lingers in the distance.
The time has come at last
for me to hold her precious gems,
true treasures from her past.

But . . .

. . . Grandma has no rubies
or green em'ralds I can hold.

There are no shiny silver coins.
There's nothing made of gold.

Instead,
she places on my head
a veil all white with pearls.

She reaches,
brushes back my hair.
She tucks away
my curls.

And then she smiles
when she recalls
one gorgeous summer day,

the day when Grandma
wore this veil
and held her small bouquet.

And though it was
so long ago
when she became
his bride,

my Grandpa still
will take her hand
when she is at his side.

Then eyes of blue
look far away
as she remembers when,

he'd write to her love letters
that she's reading
now again.

And when she smiles
I take a peek.
He wrote his love was true,

and all these letters
they are bound
with ribbons that are blue.

Then Grandma holds
a special gift.
She says, "I still enjoy

the memory of
one Mother's Day,
that's when my little boy,

he made this special card
for me.
He said he was so glad

to be my son,
and I am proud
that boy is now your dad."

I listen, watch, go back in time.
A closeness fills the air,
a feeling of discovery as I listen to her share

old stories from a cherished past,

a time when she was young,
a barefoot girl who danced in fields
to songs that once were sung.

forget-me-not

And now she holds within her hand
a necklace she has worn
for many years and long before
the day that I was born.

"A special gift," my Grandma says,
"received so long ago,
a gift that I now give to you.
Remember as you grow,

to look for treasures in your life
in simple things you see,
to love, believe, have faith, become
what you were meant to be.

And may this gift throughout the years
remind you, help renew,
the blessing of this special day
and all I've shared with you."

My Grandma smiles. I won't forget
the lessons learned today.
And as I grow, her gift I'll wear.
I'm grateful, proud to say

daisy

that yes,
she is a part of me.
I'm rich because I'm sure,

some treasures in this life are found
in Grandmas just like her.

Make Your Own Sweet Treasure Chest

This is a great activity for all grandchildren
(including grandsons)
to do with Grandma on a cold or rainy afternoon.

Things You Will Need:

1. An old shoebox or other kind of box big enough to store your treasures.
2. Paper to cover the box, scissors, tape
3. Crayons or colored pencils
4. Stickers are optional (that means if you want to)
5. Your treasures

Next:

1. Cover your box with paper. Your Grandma can help judge how much paper you will need.
   Cut carefully with scissors.
2. Tape paper securely to your box.
3. Using crayons or colored pencils, write your name on top of your box, for example:
   Ellen's or Maddie's or Gabriella's or Maggie's
   or
   Ethan's or Gavin's or Murray's or Gibson's Treasures
   (you get the idea)
4. Decorate the outside of your box with stickers and artwork created by you and your Grandma.
5. On the inside cover it is a good idea to write: "Made with Grandma on this Day" and then put the date.
6. Gather your treasures, for example: pictures of your family, your own priceless artwork, birthday cards and anything else that has special meaning for you. Place these treasures carefully in your box.
7. Cover your treasure chest with the covered box top. Store in a safe place.
8. NEVER throw it away. Keep it all your life.
9. Be sure to add any other treasures as time goes on.

Remember:

True treasures are the ones that warm your heart with happy memories!